The Colorful World of Monica
A Doggie Adventure
A bilingual book

El colorido mundo de Mónica
Una aventura perruna

Un libro bilingüe

Written by María Mercedes Rodríguez
Illustrated by Gerardo Rodríguez
Story by María Mercedes Rodríguez, Gerardo Rodríguez, and Juan Agustín Márquez

Edited by Isidra Mencos
Photographs by Juan Agustín Márquez

"I think it's coming from over there!" cried Monica as she ran toward the tree trunk. Monica couldn't believe her eyes! Four dogs! She had never seen such colorful and cool dogs before.

"¡Creo que el sonido viene de ahí!", exclamó mientras corría hacia un tronco caído. Mónica no se lo podía creer. ¡Cuatro perritos! Nunca había visto unos perritos tan coloridos y chulos.

Monica always picked up sticks on her walk
and brought them home to build forts.
But she thought of a better use for this stick.
"Fetch!" yelled Monica as she threw the stick in the air,
so Buddy could fetch it. The other dogs explored while
Buddy played fetch with Monica.

Mónica siempre recogía palitos durante su caminata y
se los llevaba a casa para construir castillos. Pero ahora se le ocurrió
un uso mejor. **"¡Búscalo!"**, gritó Mónica, y tiró el palito para que Buddy lo atrapara.
Mientras los demás perros exploraban, Buddy jugó con Mónica a buscar palitos.

As they started walking back to Monica's house, Renato took the lead and ran superfast, Mindy walked quietly beside Monica, Buddy carried the stick they'd been playing with in his humongous mouth, and Sierra smelled all the flowers along the way.

De camino a casa, Renato iba adelante corriendo súper rápido, Mindy caminaba despacio y calladamente al lado de Mónica, Buddy traía el palito con el que estaban jugando en su boca grandota, y Sierra olía todas las flores a su alrededor.

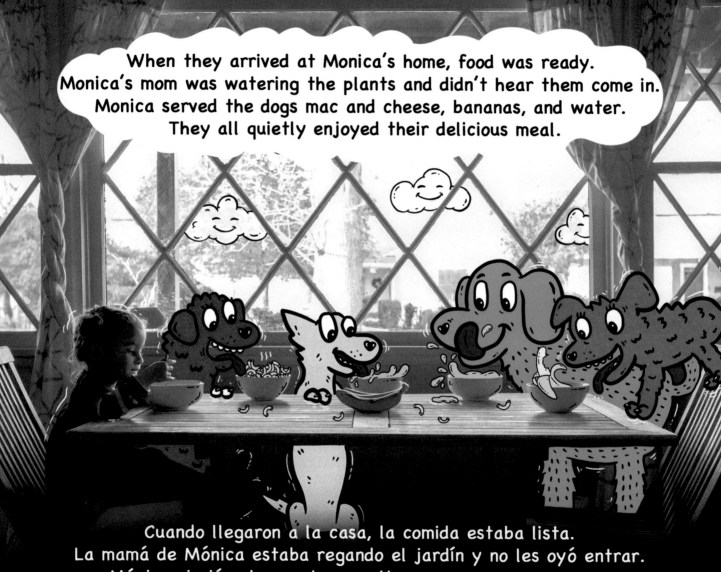

When they arrived at Monica's home, food was ready.
Monica's mom was watering the plants and didn't hear them come in.
Monica served the dogs mac and cheese, bananas, and water.
They all quietly enjoyed their delicious meal.

Cuando llegaron a la casa, la comida estaba lista.
La mamá de Mónica estaba regando el jardín y no les oyó entrar.
Mónica sirvió a los cuatro perritos macarrones con queso,
guineos y agua.Todos disfrutaron de una comida deliciosa en silencio.

Monica's mom came in the dining room. She loved dogs and was very happy to see them all. "Monica, who are your friends?" asked her mom."Mom, these are Mindy, Renato, Buddy and Sierra. We found each other in the Enchanted Forest. They need families!" said Monica. "But who would want an adorable, kind, soft, cuddly, loyal, life companion?" asked her mom. Monica thought for a minute."I bet Grandma would!" she yelled.

La mamá de Mónica entró al comedor. A ella le encantaban los perros y cuando los vio se puso feliz. "Mónica, ¿quiénes son tus amigos?", preguntó. "Mami, estos son Mindy, Renato, Buddy y Sierra. Nos encontramos en el Bosque Encantado. ¡Necesitan familias!", dijo Mónica."Pero, ¿quién querrá un compañero de vida adorable, amable, suave, tierno y leal?", preguntó la mamá. Mónica pensó un rato. "¡Abuela!" gritó.

Monica brought Mindy
to Grandma's apartment.
As soon as Grandma saw Mindy,
her face glowed with happiness.

Mónica llevó a Mindy al apartamento de Abuela.
En cuanto vio a Mindy, la cara de Abuela se iluminó de alegría.

But what about Buddy?
He loved playing fetch in the forest.
And with that big mouth and body,
he needs plenty of space.
Our neighbors have a big house,
and they've been talking
about wanting a dog for
some time.

Pero, ¿qué voy a hacer con Buddy?
Le encantó jugar con palitos en el bosque.
Además, tiene esa boca y cuerpo enormes,
así que necesita mucho espacio.
Nuestros vecinos tienen una casa grande,
¡y siempre han dicho que quieren un perro!

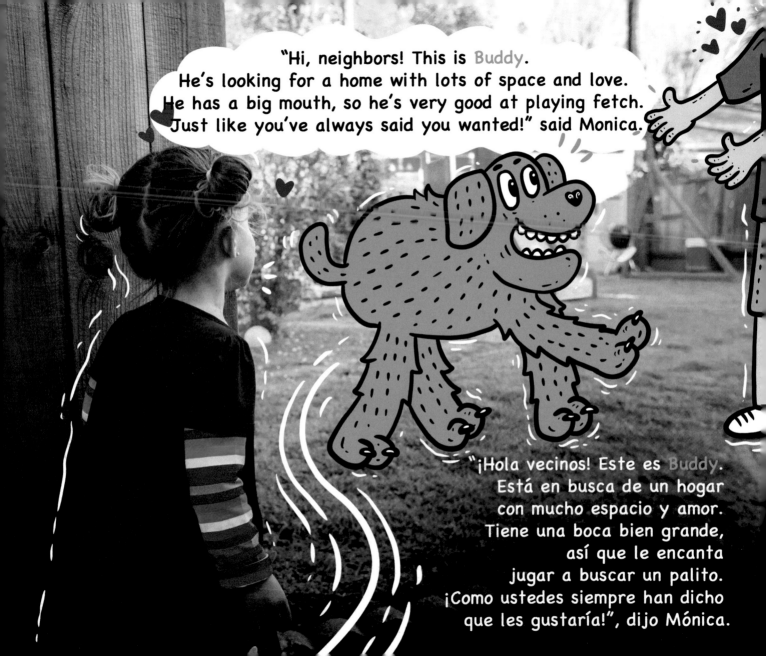

On their run, they saw Monica's aunt, who also loved to run.
"Oh, Monica, what a lovely dog!" cried Monica's aunt.
"He's looking for a home," said Monica.
"I've always wanted a running companion!" said the aunt.

Mientras corrían, vieron a la tía de Mónica,
a quien también le encantaba correr.
"Mónica, ¡qué perro más lindo!", exclamó su tía.
"Le estoy buscando un hogar", dijo Mónica.
"¡Me encantaría un compañero para correr!", dijo la tía.

And the four dogs from the Enchanted Forest found new families, thanks to Monica.

Y los cuatro perros del Bosque Encantado encontraron una familia, gracias a Mónica.

To Homer, Maruja, Cookies, and Mónica (my children in order of arrival).
You make my life whole. M.M.R.

To my best friend Titus. You will always be my inspiration. G.M.R.

Thank you to my brother Gerardo for making the most beautiful art
and joining me in this adventure;
to my daughter Mónica for being a ray of sunshine and inspiring me every day;
to my husband Juan for all of your help, unconditional support, and everlasting love;
to my dogs for making me a dog mommy;
to my parents for your wholehearted love and support.
Thank you Isidra Mencos for helping me write my first book.
Thank you Maritere Bellas for your advice.

ADOPT, DON'T SHOP. SPAY AND NEUTER.

Contact us at: TheColorfulWorldOfMonica@gmail.com
Copyright 2019
ISBN 9781092886390
Independently Published

Made in the USA
Columbia, SC
11 May 2019